**Clifford's Puppy days**

# LEAF SEASON

**By Quinlan B. Lee**

**Illustrated by Barry Goldberg**

**Based on the Scholastic book series "Clifford The Big Red Dog" by Norman Bridwell**

ISBN 0-439-67048-9

10 9 8 7 6 5 4 3 2 1          04 05 06 07 08

Designed by John Daly

Printed in the U.S.A.    First printing, September 2004

**SCHOLASTIC INC.**

New York    Toronto    London    Auckland    Sydney
Mexico City    New Delhi    Hong Kong    Buenos Aires

Before Clifford was a Big Red Dog, he was a tiny red puppy. He lived in an apartment in the city with Emily Elizabeth and her parents.

Clifford loved life with the Howards.

Most of all, Clifford loved being with Emily Elizabeth.

On a walk one day, Clifford was surprised
when a big orange leaf dropped on him.

"Look, the leaves are changing colors," said Emily Elizabeth. "That means summer's over. Now it's fall."

Clifford didn't want anything to change.
He liked everything the way it was.

"Clifford, why are you so sad?" asked Mrs. Sidarsky.
"I don't want the seasons to change," replied Clifford. "I love summer and picnics and eating yummy treats with my friends."

"Cheer up, Clifford!" squeaked the littlest Sidarsky. "There are lots of yummy treats in the fall, too — juicy apples, pumpkin cookies, and pecan pies. Delicious!"

Inside the apartment, Clifford saw a bag of towels and beach toys by the door. His tail wagged happily.

Then Mrs. Howard picked up the bag and
put it on a high closet shelf.
Clifford hid under the rug.

"What's wrong?" asked Daffodil, peeking under the rug.

"I thought we were going swimming," said Clifford, "but then Mrs. Howard came and put the beach bag away."

"It's too cold to go swimming now," explained Daffodil. "She put the bag away until next summer."

"Wait and see, Clifford," said Daffodil. "There are lots of other fun things to do in the fall."

Norville landed on the Howards' windowsill. "What are you wearing?" Clifford asked him. "A scarf," replied the bird. "The wind was blowing, and I was chilly."

"Don't you miss the warm summer sun?" asked Clifford.

"Sometimes," chirped Norville. "But I love to fly and play in the wind."

The wind blew lots of leaves down, and soon there were huge piles everywhere. Clifford had a great time pouncing into the leaf piles and rolling around with Flo and Zo. Maybe his friends were right about fall fun!

When Jorge came outside, everyone played hide-and-seek.
Clifford found the perfect hiding place.

That afternoon, Clifford and Emily Elizabeth walked to the park.
Clifford loved how the colorful leaves danced on the sidewalk.

The cool autumn breeze felt good on
the puppy's face, but it made him shiver.

Emily Elizabeth picked him up and snuggled him in her jacket. Clifford felt warm and happy. *It's fun that some things change,* he thought.

But he loved that other things stayed exactly the same!